The Worry Tree

The Worry Tree

Marianne Musgrove

Henry Holt and Company ✎ New York

Henry Holt and Company, LLC
Publishers since 1866
175 Fifth Avenue
New York, New York 10010
www.HenryHoltKids.com

Library of Congress Cataloging-in-Publication Data
Musgrove, Marianne.
The Worry Tree / Marianne Musgrove.—1st American ed.
p.   cm.
Summary: Juliet is a worrier, but when constant bickering between her and her
younger sister leads Juliet to move into her own bedroom, she discovers the Worry
Tree her grandmother used as a girl to relieve her own concerns.
ISBN-13: 978-0-8050-8791-8 / ISBN-10: 0-8050-8791-5
[1. Worry—Fiction.   2. Sisters—Fiction.   3. Grandmothers—Fiction.
4. Family life—Australia—Fiction.   5. Schools—Fiction.
6. Australia—Fiction.]   I. Title.
PZ7.M9693Wor 2008   [Fic]—dc22   2007046944

First American Edition—2008
Printed in the United States of America on acid-free paper. ∞
1   3   5   7   9   10   8   6   4   2

Dedicated to my grandparents—
Margar, who told me stories,
and Jim, who encouraged me to write them

Juliet Jennifer Jones opened the door, stepped out of the bathroom, and walked straight into her little sister.

"Eight minutes and forty-seven seconds," said Ophelia, clicking her stopwatch. "What *were* you doing in there?"

"Mom!" shrieked Juliet. "Oaf's timing me in the bathroom again!"

When there was no reply, Juliet stomped out of the room.

Ophelia, also known as Oaf, smiled quietly to herself, pulled out a yellow pad of paper, and carefully wrote *8:47* in the left-hand column. Then she tucked the notepad back into her pocket and went off to find her sister.

Juliet stormed through the house looking for an adult. She went into the living room, but Mom had her nose in her favorite Shakespearean play.

"Give me five more minutes," said Mom, "and then I will speak to thee, I mean, I'll speak to you."

Juliet rolled her eyes and went in search of Dad.

Dad was in the laundry making a model volcano, and she couldn't get him to talk about anything other than lava, ash, or explosions. She frowned and went in search of Nana.

Nana lived in the apartment down in the back garden, but when Juliet got there, all she found was a note taped to the door: *Gone to craft class. This week: macramé pot holders!*

Juliet turned around, huffing. Oaf was standing behind her singing a song she'd learned on the playground that week. It was called "The Irritating Song," and you just kept chanting it over and over like this:

> *Irritating, irritating,*
> *Irritating-tating-tating,*
> *It's the song you'll end up hating*
> *Just 'cause it's so irritating.*

That was the first verse. The second verse went like this:

> *So frustrating, so frustrating,*
> *So frustrating-strating-strating,*
> *It's the song you'll end up hating*
> *Just 'cause it's so* [clap] *frustrating.*

The other twenty-two verses continued on in pretty much the same vein. Oaf really liked that song.

"Irritating, irritating . . ."

Juliet gritted her teeth. She could feel her skin itching and prickling.

Oh, no, she thought. It's starting again.

Juliet was cursed with a nervous rash, which flared up whenever she was stressed. It started shortly after Oaf was born (no coincidence as far as Juliet was concerned) and had continued on and off for the last seven years.

"Irritating-tating-tating . . ."

Juliet ducked past her sister, down the long hallway, past the Room That Must Be Locked When Visitors Come, and into the bedroom she shared with Oaf. She shut the door firmly behind her and sank down on the floor. Now she was safe. Sort of. She gazed up at a sign on her wall. Mom had made it especially for her. I AM A CAPA-BLE PERSON WHO CAN HANDLE ANY CRISIS, it said. Juliet said these words over and over when she was feeling upset. She tried to say them now, but Oaf was singing on the other side of the door and it was putting her off.

"It's the song you'll end up hating . . ."

Juliet bit her thumbnail. Didn't she have enough to worry about? Dad always in a muddle, Mom working long hours, Nana refusing to wear her safety alarm. . . . It was extremely hard work running a family when you were only ten. And then there was Hugh Allen. . . .

"Just 'cause it's so irritating . . ."

Juliet's rash spread like foot soldiers, straight up her arms and back down her legs. She had to do something before she was driven completely mad. There was only one thing for it.

Sorting. That's what Juliet did to relax. While others lit candles, played music, and took warm baths, Juliet sorted through the many strange collections she kept in her bedroom. For the record, she owned

+ an eraser collection (143 in total);
+ a dried-cicada-shell collection (numbering fifty-one);
+ a book filled with license plate numbers (any car that parked in Juliet's street was recorded in this book);
+ ribbons for perfect attendance at school (twelve at last count);

+ a box of used bus tickets (sixty-seven as of Tuesday);

+ Piranha, her Venus flytrap.

She also had a row of tiny cactus plants she'd been collecting since the spring. She liked the way they kept growing even without the rain. She liked the way they managed on their own.

Juliet pulled out a bright blue box. Written on the lid in thick silver marker were her initials: JJJ, just like three fishhooks in a row. Juliet kept her collection of teeth inside, lying on white cotton wool, just so they'd be comfortable.

How should I sort them today? she wondered. Color (white, whitish yellow, yellowish white, gray), shape (fat and square, sharp and pointy, those with fillings, those with holes), or owner (Dad, Oaf, herself, or her best friend, Lindsay)?

She sat down on the carpet, crossed her legs neatly, and balanced the box on her lap. "I think shape," she said. She took hold of the lid and lifted it up. She looked inside. The teeth were

not there! Juliet's mind raced to one grim con-
clusion: "Oaf!"

Shortly afterward, Mom found the two sisters
arguing in the bedroom.

"Why can't you leave my things alone?"

"Mm?" said Oaf.

"I know you took my teeth."

"Teeth?"

"Yes, teeth! The ones from my collection!"

"Ohhhh, thoooose," said Oaf. "I borrowed
them to make a set of false teeth."

"What?!"

"With some modeling clay."

"Oaf!"

"And some Super Glue."

Juliet's skin itched like mad. She let out a
long, loud shriek.

"All right, girls," said Mom. "No more fighting today. It's not helpful."

As a psychologist, Mom had a great understanding of Conflict and Sibling Rivalry, which
is another way of saying fights between sisters.

"But, Mom—" began Juliet.

"I mean it, you two. Shouting and screaming won't solve a thing. I think it's time the three of us sat down and talked things through."

Juliet and Oaf groaned. Talking Things Through was never a pleasant experience.

"I reckon she's going to make us Name Our Feelings," muttered Oaf.

Please, no, thought Juliet.

"I've been thinking things over," said Mom, "and I've decided we should all name our feelings."

Oaf raised an eyebrow. "Told you," she said.

The girls had been through this naming exercise before. The idea was to say things like "I feel X when you do Y." For example, "I feel *angry* when you lick all the cookies, then put them back in the package" (message from Juliet to Oaf) or "I feel *frustrated* when you follow me around with binoculars taking notes" (another message from Juliet to Oaf).

"So, girls," said Mom, looking from one daughter to the other, "who wants to go first? Anyone? Anyone at all? No? Well, all right then, why don't I start things off?"

Mom settled herself on the carpet and folded her hands. "When you girls fight and shout at each other, I feel upset and frazzled, and the noise makes me feel tense and unhappy. Now," she said, turning to Juliet, "what do you have to share with us, Worrywart?"

Oaf pricked up her ears. "Juliet has warts? We should probably all wear flip-flops in the shower."

Juliet's skin throbbed. She was very, very tired of Oaf and her so-called Humor. Maybe it *was* time she named some of her feelings.

"When Oaf," she said, looking down at the empty box, "takes my things without asking, again and again and again and again, I *feel* like punching her in the face."

"Juliet!" said Mom. "That's not in the spirit of the exercise."

Juliet crossed her arms.

"All right, then. Oaf," said Mom, "you name your feelings."

Ophelia looked thoughtful.

"Wendy and Brian," she said.

"Very funny, Oaf," said Mom, looking exasperated. "You know that's not what I meant. I think we'll skip the naming exercise today. What you two really need are your own rooms."

"Really?" said Juliet. "But doesn't that mean—"

"Yes," said Mom. "It does. Hold on to your hats, girls!"

Juliet wondered how long she would have to hold on to her hat. Twenty-four hours had passed, and so far nothing had happened. She decided to check her To Do list in order to keep calm.

Clean teeth—ten seconds per tooth ✓

Brush hair—100 times ✓

Put on Sunday underwear, Sunday sandals, Sunday T-shirt, and Sunday shorts ✓

Put Band-Aids on fingers to stop biting nails ✓

Find Oaf—remove stopwatch ✓

Eat breakfast—100 cornflakes, one glass of milk ✓

Make sure Nana hasn't fallen over in the
  night ✓
Tidy sock drawer ✓
Feed Piranha

"Right," said Juliet. "Time for Piranha's lunch."

"Need me to catch some flies?" said Oaf. She could often be found stalking around the house crouched low with a plastic flyswatter raised above her head.

Juliet nodded. There were never enough flies in their bedroom. Her Venus flytrap was very fond of them. More a pet than a plant, Piranha would sit still, waiting to pounce, then the moment a fly landed in one of his traps—*snap!*—it was gone. There was something exciting about having a dangerous creature living in your bedroom.

"Some more supplies'd be good," said Juliet.

"That'll be ten cents a fly."

"It used to be five!"

"The dollar isn't what it used to be," said Oaf,

climbing off her bed. As she looked for her fly-swatter, a burst of loud talking came from the hallway.

"Do I have to, Karen? Really? Please don't make me do it!"

Uh-oh, thought Juliet. It's begun.

The girls went out to investigate. As expected, they found Dad standing in front of the door of the Room That Must Be Locked When Visitors Come. His long, thin arms and legs were stretched out as if he were doing a star jump. Mom was tugging on his sleeve.

"Martin," said Mom, "come on, now. I just want to take a look."

Dad gripped the doorframe.

"Come on, love."

The Room That Must Be Locked When Visitors Come happened to be Dad's study. Taped to the door was a large sheet of paper bearing the words of Thomas Edison: TO INVENT, YOU NEED A GOOD IMAGINATION AND A PILE OF JUNK. Inside was the pile of junk. There were specimen jars with dead things inside, piles of old boxes and milk crates, a broken telescope, blown light-bulbs, empty fruit juice cartons, and cans of dried paint. There was so much stuff in there you had to suck your stomach in just so you could move between the towers of boxes. And every-thing was covered in a layer of dust—a thick, gray fur that made Juliet think of hibernating bears. At night, she imagined their great, warm bodies stirring in the dark.

"Martin," said Mom, "I can't bear that junk anymore. We can't have guests over; I have to hide it from my mother . . ."

Juliet agreed with Mom. Mess meant stress. Oaf, on the other hand, could be found regularly organizing tours for the local neighborhood children. They came in order to be shocked by the sort of mess *their* mothers would never allow. They never went home disappointed.

"Think about it," said Mom. "If Juliet doesn't get her own room soon, we'll have a murder on our hands."

Juliet tensed. She didn't want to be the reason for a fight between her parents.

"But what about my scientific research?" said Dad.

"Research?" said Mom. "Please explain to me how three hundred margarine containers filled with rubber bands counts as research."

Mom's and Dad's voices got louder. Oaf leaned against Juliet for comfort, and Juliet, though three years older, leaned back. She wished she'd stayed in the bedroom and searched for flies. She wasn't ready to be a Child of Divorce.

"Please, Martin," said Mom. "Please."

"Well . . . ," said Dad.

Dad always knew when he was beaten, and the following weekend, the big cleanup began. It was a day of dust and dirt and sore backs, and by four o'clock it was time for a break outside.

"Mom," said Juliet, putting down her juice with a glassy clunk, "can I invite Lindsay over to see my new room?"

Mom set aside the play she was reading. "Of course," she said. "It should be ready in about two weeks. New paint, new carpet, new bed, the lot."

"Could I invite Gemma too?"

"I don't know a Gemma. Is she a new friend of yours?"

"Yes," said Juliet. "Well, no. I haven't met her yet, but I've seen her at school."

"Anyone's welcome in our home," said Dad, crossing his long, bendy legs.

"If they don't touch my maggot farm," said Oaf.

Juliet was about to explain that no one in their right mind would want to touch Oaf's maggot farm when Nana appeared in the doorway of her apartment. "Thought I smelled muffins," she said.

She walked up the path wearing a red dress with a long string of black beads around her neck. She used a stick to steady herself, and Juliet noticed how long it took her to reach the veranda.

"I thought you were supposed to be at craft class," said Juliet. "Making fridge magnets out of matchsticks or something."

"Yes," said Nana, "but there are only so many fridge magnets an ex–university professor can make before she starts going crazy."

"Muffin?" said Dad, holding out a plate.

"Actually," said Nana, heaving herself up the step, "I think I'll pass on the muffins. My real reason for skipping class was to take a look at my old bedroom before it's redecorated. Coming, Juliet?"

Juliet followed her gladly. Oaf had been singing "The Irritating Song" and was already up to verse seventeen.

Number 23 Gregson Street was more than a hundred years old, built by Nana's great-grandfather. It was made of big yellow sandstone blocks, and the doors were as thick as the Yellow Pages. Juliet liked the windows best, especially the round one in the front door. It was a greeny blue color and looked like a puddle after a stone's been thrown in the middle. When you peered through it, the people on the other side looked as if they were underwater.

"I didn't realize my new bedroom used to be your old bedroom," said Juliet.

"I slept in there when I was a girl," said Nana, "about your age. Later, it became a kind of store-room. Then I moved into the apartment when your parents got married."

They walked down the hallway until they

came to the old study door. The quote from Thomas Edison lay crumpled on the floor: TO INVENT, YOU NEED . . . but the rest of the words were hidden from view. Nana pushed open the door, and in they went, stirring up dust with every step. The room smelled of damp newspaper and old books, and there were cracks in the wall you could fit your hand inside. Juliet noticed the wallpaper peeling off in several places. She took a step closer.

"This is unbelievable," said Nana. "It's like stepping into the past."

Juliet tugged at a curling strip of wallpaper. It was just like peeling a large, papery banana, and it felt very satisfying. She reached up and tore off another piece.

Then she saw it.

"Nana!" she said, ripping off more paper. "Nana!"

Strips of torn paper lay curling in piles on the floor, looking like enormous pencil shavings. Beneath the wallpaper was a painting of a tree, its branches stretching out along the wall like a climbing rose. Juliet scrunched up her nose at the dust and leaned forward.

"Look at this!" she said. "There are animals in the branches. I can see a wombat, a peacock, a dog, a pig, a goat, and a duck."

Juliet stepped back to get a better look. The colors of the tree had faded to dusty cinnamons, tea browns, and soft olive greens, and the colors of the animals, which must once have been bright, were now watery blues, lemony yellows, and pale rose pinks.

"Well!" said Nana. "I know this tree. I know it very well." She flipped the catch on her walking stick, and it opened out into a three-legged stool. "I need to sit down," she added, lowering herself onto the seat, "to take it all in."

"How did it get here?" said Juliet. "How? When? Why was it covered up?"

Nana fingered the beads around her neck, her mind far away. At last, she lifted a bony finger and pointed at the wall. "Look at these words," she said. "Here, down at the bottom."

Tangled in among the roots were some letters, a message looping and coiling like a single curl of apple peel. THE WORRY TREE, it said.

"What's a Worry Tree?" said Juliet. "Is it magic?"

"No, it's not magic," said Nana. "Not magic at all."

"Oh," said Juliet, disappointed.

"But," said Nana, "just because something's not magic doesn't mean it can't be magical."

Juliet thought about this for a moment. Not magic, but magical. Like her imagination, maybe?

"So, if it's not magic, how does it work?"

"You hang your worries on the tree each night so they don't keep you awake."

"How? What do you mean?"

"Start by thinking of something that's worrying you. Maybe someone you know is making life hard for you."

Hugh Allen, thought Juliet.

"Imagine that worry sitting in the palm of your hand, like this." Nana held out her hand as though she were cupping something. "Imagine an invisible string tied around its middle with a loop on top, like a Christmas tree decoration. Then take hold of the loop between your thumb and forefinger and hang it on one of the branches of the Worry Tree, like this," she said and reached up and touched the end of a branch, pretending to hang her worry on it. "The Worry Tree animals will look after your worries till morning comes. In other words, they do the worrying for you while you sleep."

"Wow!" said Juliet. "What else?"

"The wombat," replied Nana, pointing at the

hairy-nosed creature, "is named . . . Wolfgang. That's right, Wolfgang. And when I was worried about any of my friends, I'd ask him to help me out. It was his job, you see?"

"How come?"

"All the animals in the Worry Tree have special jobs. The dog—his name's Dimitri—he worries about family, and the pig, over here, worries about school."

"What's her name?"

Nana paused to think. "Petronella," she said at last. "Petronella, the pig. Then there's Gwyneth, the goat, for when you're feeling sick. She's good with tummy bugs and chicken pox and broken bones. And then there's the peacock, who's in charge of minding worries about things you've lost. That could mean a necklace or some money or even a pet."

"And what's he called?" asked Juliet, gazing at the pale blue feathers fanning out behind him.

"Piers," said Nana. "And last of all, there's that little white duck sitting on the bottom branch." Nana tapped the wall. It looked as though the duck was ruffling its feathers. "Her name's Delia. She knows it's hard to get used to change, so she looks after that kind of thing."

"What kind of thing?"

"Changing schools, changing houses, even changing bedrooms. All those things take a bit of getting used to."

Juliet felt stirred up. There was something terribly mysterious about having an ancient painting hidden away in your bedroom. She wondered if a bit of the mystery would rub off on her.

"Oh!" said Nana. "I almost forgot. See that black hole painted on the tree trunk?"

"Yes."

"That's where you put the worries you can't describe. You know, those times when you feel bad and you don't know why. That black hole is there to catch all the extra problems the animals don't look after. You just put those worries in the hole as if you're posting a letter."

"Wow!" said Juliet. She was amazed that such a tree had existed in her house all these years, a tree so secret she'd never, ever known about it. Until now.

"So how did it get here?" she asked.

"No one knows for sure," said Nana, "but the story I heard was that your great-great-grandmother—my mother's mother—painted it when she was a girl. That was over one hundred years ago. She was the eldest child in the family and famous for being a worrywart."

"So it runs in the family!" said Juliet, relieved she wasn't the only one. "But, Nana, why's it all covered up?"

Nana sighed, her eyes tearing up. "It's a bit of a sad story," she said. "Would you like to hear it?"

"My father did it," said Nana. "My father papered over the Worry Tree."

"But why?" said Juliet. She couldn't understand how any father could be so mean.

"My mother took me to Melbourne to visit my grandmother, and while we were away, my father had all my toys removed and my room redecorated. He thought I was getting too old for childish games. He said he did it for my own good."

"That must've been really bad," said Juliet. "To lose your Worry Tree friends like that."

"It was," said Nana. "For a while there, I felt quite lost."

"But now they're back," said Juliet.

"Yes," said Nana. "They're back to help the latest generation."

Over the next few days, Juliet thought a lot about the Worry Tree. She was thinking about it when her best friend, Lindsay, nudged her in the ribs and waved a hand in front of her face.

"Juliet," she said, "Juliet, are you listening? I was just asking if you've got a question for us today?"

Juliet reached into her bag and pulled out her lunch box. Written on the lid in thick gray marker were her initials: JJJ, just like three monkey tails in a row. Whenever Dad made lunch, he popped in a scientific question for the girls to talk about. They were usually questions like *Why does cold chicken taste different from hot chicken?* or *Why is yawning contagious?*

Juliet read out today's question. "Fish have their eyes stuck on either side of their heads. What would happen if humans did?"

"Good question," said Lindsay, and she pushed her hair out of her eyes and put on her thinking face. She was one of those people born with mad-scientist hair. She didn't mind, though, as she had every intention of becoming a scientist when she grew up, though hopefully not a mad one. "If I had fish eyes," she said, "I wouldn't have to turn my head to the left or right when I crossed the street. I could see the cars coming both ways at the same time!"

"A referee could watch both ends of the field during a soccer game," added Juliet.

"And people could cheat on their exams by looking at their neighbors' answers."

"Yes!" said Juliet and shook her head at the idea of all that cheating. As she put the thought out of her mind, she noticed the new girl sitting by herself.

Gemma had a pretty face, plump and creamy white like a scoop of ice cream. Freckles tumbled off the bridge of her nose like spilled sesame seeds, and her hair was the color of nutmeg. Her teeth were square and straight and looked like a row of sugar cubes. Juliet knew at once what people meant when they said someone looked good enough to eat. The new girl was positively delicious.

"See that girl over there?" said Juliet, knowing it was a risk to interrupt Lindsay when she was Deep in Thought.

"Mm?" said Lindsay. "Oh. Her."

"Do you think we should ask her to sit with us?"

"I don't know," said Lindsay. "We might not like her. And anyway, we've got other things to worry about."

"Like what?"

"Like the fact that Hugh Allen is coming our way."

Hugh was famous for being the biggest bully at Wattle Street School. He was also famous for having the biggest nostrils in the school. People said they'd gotten that big from all the marbles he'd stuck up there. All Juliet knew was that the sight of him made her skin prickle.

"Hi, Jooly-Wooly," said the boy. "Ooh, what's that?" He reached out and snatched Juliet's lunch box from her hands. "Urgh," he said. "Health food." He unwrapped her sandwich and tossed it on the ground. Lettuce, tomato, and beets scattered on the concrete.

Juliet looked at Lindsay for backup, but Lindsay was staring at her apple as if it were the most interesting apple in the whole world.

"Oh, look," said Hugh. "Snotberry yogurt!" He ripped off the lid and tipped Juliet's yogurt straight down his throat in one noisy gulp. "Got anything else?"

Juliet's rash bloomed all over her body like itchy flowers. "Get lost," she whispered, wishing she could think of something better to say.

"What's that?"

"Go away."

"But we're best friends," said Hugh. "Don't you want to talk to your best friend?"

"You're not my best friend," said Juliet. "Lindsay is." She looked over at her friend, but Lindsay was still staring at her apple. Juliet felt a small pain in her chest, as if she were being jabbed with a thumbtack. She pulled off one of her Band-Aids and started chewing her nail.

"Looks like I *am* your best friend," said Hugh, picking up her bag and tipping it upside down. "Your only friend."

As he kicked her things across the asphalt, Juliet's heart sank. What was she going to do now?

"Hey!" called a voice. "Hey!"

Juliet, Lindsay, and Hugh looked up.

"I want to talk to you!"

The voice belonged to Gemma. She strode toward them, her nutmeg hair shimmering in the sun, her creamy ice cream skin stained an angry raspberry red. It looked as if she was holding something behind her back.

"Yeah?" said Hugh, dropping Juliet's bag. "What do you want?"

Gemma stared at him steadily, eyeball to eyeball, then she leaned in close—very, very close.

"I want to show you something," she said. "But first, I have to warn you, it's pretty scary. You might not be able to handle it."

"Huh!" said Hugh. "I can handle anything."

"Oh, I don't know," said Gemma. "There have

been people before you—tougher people—who haven't been able to cope. Some even had to have counseling."

"I'm not scared," said Hugh. "Just show it to me, will you?"

Very slowly, Gemma brought her hand around from behind her back. Juliet watched hopefully, wondering what this menacing thing could be. When Gemma held out the object, Juliet's hopes were dashed. Oh, no, she thought. We're all doomed.

"A doll!" Hugh laughed. "Is that it? Oooh, I'm so scared. I can't believe you still play with dolls."

"Oh, this isn't just any doll," said Gemma calmly. "This is Xtreme Sportz Bettina. And I don't carry her around to play with. I use her as a weapon. On boys just like you."

"Whatever you say," said Hugh. "It's still just a doll."

Gemma smiled patiently. "Did I mention Xtreme Sportz Bettina comes with a range of rather nasty accessories?"

"Accessories?" said Hugh, his voice wavering slightly. "What kind of accessories?"

"You don't want to know," said Gemma. "Let's just say they cause quite a bit of discomfort." And she thrust the doll into the air as if brandishing a sword.

Juliet looked at Lindsay with wide eyes. This was more exciting than a nature documentary!

"By the way," said Gemma, "did I mention three kids from my old school have restraining orders out against me? That means I'm not allowed to come within five hundred yards of them if I'm 'in possession of my Bettina doll.' That's how scared they are."

Hugh looked as though he couldn't decide whether Gemma was serious or not. Then Gemma shoved the doll in his face and removed all doubt.

"Yeah, well, I've got stuff to do," he said, stepping backward. "Haven't got time to stand around playing with dolls." And he walked very quickly across the playground.

"Thanks," said Juliet, laughing with relief. "Thanks for that."

"No problem," said Gemma, flashing her sugar-cube smile. "Actually, I kind of enjoyed it."

Lindsay sniffed and looked the other way, but Juliet was too happy to notice.

All in all, thought Juliet, it had been an unusual day. Hugh had been defeated, and now she was about to spend her first night in her new bedroom. She looked down at her To Do list to see what tasks she had to do before bedtime.

Make sure all doors and windows are
  locked ✓
Straighten pictures in bedroom ✓
Recheck all doors and windows ✓
Check Piranha for aphids and other
  parasites ✓
Sharpen pencils for tomorrow ✓
Brush teeth and tongue, floss ✓
Change into pajamas

The idea of changing in front of the Worry Tree animals seemed embarrassing to Juliet, so she climbed under the blanket and changed out of sight. Just as she finished, there was a tapping at the door.

"It's only us," said Mom, "come to say good night."

Dad's boxes were still stacked up in the hallway, so Mom, Dad, and Oaf had to struggle over them to get inside the room. Then Dad lifted Nana up and over the boxes before she could object.

"You will clear that stuff away soon, won't you, Martin?" said Mom.

"Of course!" said Dad, and they all piled onto Juliet's new bed in a kind of affectionate tangle.

"We've got presents," said Dad. "To celebrate your new room."

"Really?" Juliet said and watched as Dad pulled a package out from under his sweater.

"It's a label maker," said Mom. "So you can print out all the labels your heart desires."

"Thanks, Mom! Thanks, Dad!" said Juliet, hugging her parents. "It's the best."

"Me next!" said Oaf, and handed over a parcel wrapped in newspaper.

Juliet unwrapped it slowly and pulled out an old gray sock with "O. Jones" written on the heel.

"His name is Pong," said Oaf. "I'm giving him to you so you won't miss me."

"Thanks," said Juliet uncertainly. "That's very . . . thoughtful." She got up quickly and sealed it in a Ziploc bag.

"The last gift's from me," said Nana. "I came across it in one of your dad's boxes."

Juliet reached out and took it. It was a small frame containing an old black-and-white photograph of a girl.

"Recognize her?" said Nana.

Juliet looked more closely. The girl was sitting in a bedroom, looking at a painting of a tree on the wall.

"It looks like me," said Juliet, "except it can't be. The photo's too old."

"That's because it's not you," said Nana. "It's—"

"You!"

"As a little girl," said Nana.

"It looks like you're talking to the tree on the wall."

"Yes," said Nana. "It does."

Once everyone had kissed Juliet good night and left the room, she was surprised to find she felt rather lonely. There was no mess covering the floor, no irritating songs were being sung, and it felt strange without Oaf on the bottom bunk, kicking her from under the mattress. How would she ever get to sleep?

Juliet climbed out of bed and sat cross-legged on the floor. The yellowy green carpet spread out across the room like a windblown wheatfield, leading to the foot of the Worry Tree. Six strong branches spread out along the wall, just as if they'd grown there. Juliet liked the idea of nature creeping quietly indoors and taking root. Not many people had a garden growing in their bedroom.

The Worry Tree animals seemed to be stirring

from their daytime sleep, ready to hear her troubles.

"Delia," she said, talking to the little white duck, "Nana says you look after changes in people's lives. I've just changed rooms, and it doesn't feel right. I feel kind of . . . uprooted."

Delia listened silently, her white feathers shimmering in the lamplight. Juliet got the feeling Delia was used to hearing about changes in people's lives, big and little. She imagined her loneliness sitting in her hand with a piece of string tied around it. Taking the imaginary loop between thumb and forefinger, she hung it on the end of Delia's branch and felt a little lighter.

"Petronella," she said, scratching the pig's upturned nose. "Why does Hugh keep picking on me? And why can't I stand up for myself? I make up heaps of things to say when he's not around, but the moment he shows up, I can't remember any of them. If it hadn't been for Gemma today, I would've been in big trouble."

Being in charge of school worries, Petronella knew all about bullies. By the look in her eyes,

Juliet could tell she had a very low opinion of them. She hung her worries on Petronella's branch and turned to Wolfgang, the wombat.

"I'm not sure if you can help or not," she said, "but since you look after friendship worries, I wanted to talk about Lindsay." Then she explained how her oldest friend, her best friend, had let her down by not defending her.

Juliet reached up and touched the wall. Wolfgang's eyes shone like two black billiard balls. When she'd finished talking, she hung her worries on the end of his branch and felt much better—not happy exactly, but lighter, like driftwood on the surface of the sea. She climbed into bed, closed her eyes, and floated off on the tide, off into a restful sleep.

Juliet was tidying her bus ticket collection on the weekend when Oaf burst into her bedroom. "Coming through!" she cried and made straight for the Useful Box.

"What are you doing in my room?" said Juliet.

"No time to explain," said Oaf, rummaging around in the box. "Where on earth's the— found it!" She held up a large roll of tape, then dropped to the floor and commando-crawled under Juliet's new bed. Moments later, Mom appeared in the doorway holding a pair of scissors.

"Oaf," said Mom, "I know you're under there. Please come out and have your hair cut."

"It's not necessary," came the muffled reply.

"School photos are coming up," replied Mom, "and I can't have you looking like a ragamuffin."

"You can't make me!" said Oaf and wriggled farther under the bed.

A little anxious V appeared between Juliet's eyebrows. Surely not another family fight? And why did it have to be in her nice, new bedroom? She wondered what the Worry Tree animals were making of all this.

"Ophelia," said Mom, "I know that you are unhappy. Why don't you come out and tell me how you feel about it?"

There was a pause followed by "You're not going to psychologic me. I'm not tricked by your psychologicness."

Both Juliet and Oaf were familiar with Mom's Psychological Techniques for Managing Children. Oaf stayed put for a reason.

"Ophelia Octavia Jones," said Mom, trying another tack, "I'll come under there and drag you out myself if I have to!"

"I'm taping my hair to my head!"

There was the sound of tape being unwound,

followed by loud bumping noises as Oaf wrapped it all the way around her head. Mom looked at Juliet tiredly. "Would you mind awfully going first, honey?"

Juliet could tell the last thing Mom needed was a Scene. "All right, Mom," she said, proud of being the good daughter.

"Hey!" called Oaf, as Juliet headed out the door. "Could you pass me the glue?"

Juliet went into the bathroom and climbed onto the three-legged stool. Mom came in and draped a tea towel around her shoulders.

"Why do humans need haircuts?" said Juliet. "Cats don't need them. Neither do koalas."

Mom clipped the tea towel together at the front. "Better ask your father about that. He's the scientist. In the meantime, it's a burden you'll just have to bear."

Another burden, thought Juliet, remembering the list of things she'd already been told she just had to bear. She imagined these burdens as a teetering tower of teacups. She imagined herself bearing them.

"Ready?" said Mom, brandishing the scissors in the air. "Then let the games begin!"

As Mom snipped, Juliet looked at herself in the mirror. Brown hair (medium length), brown eyes (medium strength), regular-sized feet (well within her age range). Adults called her Sensible, Reliable, a Pleasure to Teach. Juliet wondered what it would be like to be Pretty, Charming, Brave. Juliet wondered what it would be like to be Gemma.

"Oops," said Mom, chewing on her bottom lip. "That's a bit lopsided, isn't it? Let's straighten that up."

Juliet looked on in dismay as Mom chopped off another quarter inch.

"Oops," repeated Mom. "Let's try that again."

Another quarter inch of hair fell to the ground.

"Oops," said Mom, standing back to get a better view. "One more time, eh?"

And a little later, "Oops."

When Juliet went back into her bedroom, her bangs were exactly half an inch long. Oaf took one look at her and dived back under the bed.

"Petronella," said Juliet, tracing the curl of the little pig's tail, "my hair hasn't grown at all since this morning. I know. I've measured it. What am I going to do? Hugh will take one look at me and hassle me all week. If I didn't have you to talk to, I don't know what I'd do."

After Juliet had hung her worries on the tree, an idea formed in her mind about how to cope with her hair. She went over to the Useful Box and peered inside. "That might just work," she said, reaching into the box. "What do you think, Petronella?"

"Ophelia, honey," said Dad, "you cannot wear a motorcycle helmet to school. The teacher wouldn't like it."

Juliet had just finished taping Band-Aids to the tips of her fingers. She came out to see what was happening. Oaf was standing on top of a box with her arms crossed, a glossy black helmet wobbling on her head.

"Mom made my hair look dumb," she said.

"You don't say," said Juliet, thinking of her own hair.

"Oaf," said Mom, "I know you're embarrassed by your hair, but it *will* grow back. In the meantime, I'm sure no one will notice."

Juliet raised an eyebrow. Surely Mom was

being overly optimistic. There were some pretty sharp-eyed people at Wattle Street School.

Dad jingled his keys and looked at his watch. "You know what?" he said. "It's chocolate night tonight, and I'm afraid only people *without* motorcycle helmets get chocolate."

Oaf slowly uncrossed her arms. "What about people wearing scarves?" she said, turning toward Juliet. "Do they get chocolate?"

Juliet reached up and touched her head. She'd hoped no one would notice. Tied around her head was a bright pink scarf covering the whole of her forehead. "That's different," she said. "I'm older, so I'm allowed."

"That doesn't sound fair," said Oaf. "Does it, Dad? Does it, Mom? I'm not taking mine off unless Juliet takes hers off."

Mom and Dad looked at Juliet in that pleading sort of way that always made her feel squirmy and guilty. She sighed heavily, reached up, and slowly pulled the scarf away.

"Juliet!" gasped Mom.

"Check it out!" said Oaf.

"Inventive," said Dad.

Running in straight lines down Juliet's forehead were heavy brown marker lines drawn to look like hair.

"Honey!" said Mom. "What on earth have you done?"

A sob escaped from Juliet's lips. "I wanted to make my bangs look longer!" she wailed. "Is it really obvious?"

"Not *really* obvious," said Dad.

"It's totally obvious," said Oaf. "You look like an idiot."

"Thank you, Ophelia," said Mom. "Don't call your sister an idiot."

Tears leaked out of Juliet's eyes and glazed her cheeks.

"Don't worry," said Mom, putting her arm around Juliet's shoulders. "We've got just enough time to scrub it off with soap and water."

"That won't work!" cried Juliet. "The marker's permanent!"

Juliet held Oaf's hand and guided her to school. It isn't easy to see when you've got a motorcycle helmet on your head. Juliet used her free hand to check that her scarf was still in place. She wondered if the Worry Tree animals would be able to handle the worry load tonight.

"Bye, Oaf," said Juliet when they reached the school gate.

"Bye," said Oaf and wandered off in the wrong direction, her arms held out in front of her. Juliet grabbed her by the shoulders and pointed her toward the classroom. "It's about twenty steps, then turn left."

By the time Juliet got to class, everyone was already seated and her teacher was standing behind his desk. Mr. Castelli was a kind, though hairy, man. He had a big, bushy beard and large ears that sprouted wiry hairs like sea anemones. Juliet thought his hairiness made him look friendly.

She walked quickly between the desks, head down, and slunk into her seat next to Lindsay.

"Nice scarf," whispered Hugh, leaning across the aisle to try and pull it off.

"Juliet," said Mr. Castelli, "you're just in time to hear about the upcoming festival. Everyone in our class is bringing along something that has to do with their favorite hobby. That could be a stamp collection or trading cards, anything you like, really—the more out there, the better. In fact, there'll be a prize for the most unusual collection."

The most unusual collection? Juliet and Lindsay looked at each other. Juliet would have a shot at that!

"All the details are here on these flyers," continued Mr. Castelli. "Juliet, will you please come up to the front and hand them out for me?"

Juliet, who had been imagining herself standing onstage and accepting the award for most unusual collection, stopped short. He wanted her to go up in front of the whole class? Normally, she loved helping out. Being helpful and learning facts were her two favorite things at school. But not today. She reached up and touched her scarf as her face grew hot.

But Mr. Castelli was waiting. Juliet got up slowly and walked to the front. She took the flyers and turned around to pass them out. She hoped Mr. Castelli wouldn't say anything. She handed out the first flyer. He said nothing. She handed out the second flyer. Still okay. She handed out the third flyer.

"Juliet," said Mr. Castelli, "you might like to take that scarf off. We don't want to break school rules, now, do we?"

"No," said Juliet, wondering why adults always said "we" when they meant "you."

Everyone in the class was staring now. Juliet looked around for support. Lindsay smiled at her. Gemma did too. Juliet reached up, feeling hot and sick, and tugged at the knot on her head. The scarf fell away with a swish.

"Juliet!"

"Scrub harder," said Juliet through gritted teeth. "I can take it."

Juliet was lying on Nana's kitchen table, her head dangling backward over the edge. Nana rubbed Juliet's forehead with an old washcloth while a big plastic basin sat on the floor beneath her head, ready to catch the drips. Only moments earlier, Oaf had been helping too, until Nana had sent her outside for making "unhelpful comments."

"So the whole class laughed at you!" said Nana. "You've got lots to tell the Worry Tree animals tonight. Just be thankful you didn't have to spend three hours at the community center being talked down to by a twenty-two-year-old activities officer with a love of finger puppets."

Juliet didn't reply. Sometimes Nana said things that didn't make sense.

"Did that Hugh boy give you a hard time?"

"Actually," said Juliet, "he wasn't too bad. Whenever he came anywhere near me, Gemma pulled out her Bettina doll and he ran for it."

"Looks like you've made a new friend," said Nana, patting Juliet's arm with a damp, soapy hand. "But I'm sorry to have to tell you, these marks aren't coming off. Think I'll go surf the Net for some ideas."

While Nana turned on the computer, Juliet jumped off the table and poked around the apartment. Many of Nana's community center craft projects lay around the room: pipe-cleaner animals, Popsicle-stick placemats, things made out of egg cartons. It was like being back in kindergarten. Then she noticed Nana's safety alarm sitting on the bookshelf and the familiar V of anxiety appeared between her eyebrows. Nana was supposed to be wearing that! It went around her neck so that if she fell over in the night and couldn't get up, she could press a button and an ambulance would come.

"Nana," she said, going into her bedroom, "why aren't you wearing this?"

"Not you too!" said Nana, turning around in her chair. "Everyone's always nagging me about that. 'Why aren't you wearing your alarm, Octavia?' 'What happens if you fall over when you're alone?' 'Who's going to rescue you?' Blah, blah, blah."

Juliet frowned. She always thought of Nana as warm and happy. Holding her was just like hugging a loaf of freshly baked bread. Today, she sounded scratchy and annoyed. It would have been more like hugging one of Juliet's cactus plants.

"Are you mad at me?" said Juliet.

"No, no, of course not, love. If anything, I'm mad at myself; mad at my own body for letting me down. I'm getting old, that's all."

"What can I do?" said Juliet.

"There's nothing you can do, love, but thanks for the offer. Now, about those marker lines. . . ."

While Nana searched for a Web site on stains, Juliet thought about how, just lately, she'd overheard Nana muttering words to herself like "useless," "washed up," and "scrap heap." Juliet wanted to scrub those words clean and change them into "happy," "jolly," and "joyful." There must be something she could do! She didn't have any ideas yet, but she was sure she'd come up with something.

"Are you sure you want to put those peas in?" said Juliet.

"Absolutely," said Dad. "They're good for you."

"But are you sure they go with beets and squid rings? Can't we use a proper recipe this time? If we used a proper recipe from a proper recipe book, we'd get a proper meal."

"It's all about experimentation, Juliet. You never know what might happen when you help me in the kitchen."

Exactly, thought Juliet. Still, there was a part of her that found the possibility of unpredictable things kind of exciting.

When Mom arrived home from work, she

came into the kitchen and hugged Dad from behind. Juliet decided to join in too, and the three of them stood there holding on to one another like a kind of human stalagmite. Juliet wished her family could always be this happy.

"Peas!" said Oaf when they sat down at the dinner table. "I hate peas."

"Bad luck, Ophelia," said Mom. "You'll just have to put up with them."

"And don't get any ideas about flushing them down the toilet," said Dad.

"But I don't like them," said Oaf.

Juliet sighed. She didn't like peas either, but she still ate them. Why couldn't Oaf just behave?

"Where's Nana?" asked Mom.

"Mucking around on the computer. She said she'd have leftovers tonight," said Dad. "But guess what? I took the whole afternoon off so I could sort through those boxes in the hall."

"Oh?" said Mom. "You spent the whole afternoon sorting them? It looks even worse than it did this morning!"

"Yeah, well, the thing is, I came across some articles on the discovery of dinosaur bones in South America and, well, you know how it is, I started reading them. That was a fascinating period in history. Did you know—"

"Martin!"

"Yes, Karen?"

"Don't speak to me in that tone of voice."

"Karen! Can't we just have a pleasant dinner conversation for once?"

"Can't you just clear the mess out of the hall for once?"

Juliet's rash flared up, and her skin itched. She tried to think of something to say to make her parents happy.

"I'm not eating these peas," said Oaf, poking them with a fork. "They're foul. P–H–O–W–L. Foul."

Juliet silently begged her sister not to make a fuss.

"Ophelia," said Mom, "think of the starving children in Africa. I'm sure they'd love to be able to eat beet, pea, and squid ring stir-fry."

"I'll get an envelope," said Oaf.

"Ophelia," said Dad.

"How do you spell 'Starving Children'?"

"Oaf!"

"Okay, okay," said Oaf. "How about I burp the alphabet instead?"

Mom and Dad put down their forks and Juliet realized they were about to have one of their famous Jones Family Blowups.

"Wait!" cried Juliet, getting to her feet. "I've got an idea! Oaf, why don't you take your peas with chocolate milk? You know, like Nana's pills?"

Before anyone could stop her, Juliet got up and filled two glasses. She set them on the table and placed a single pea on the back of her tongue. Then she took a big swig of milk and washed it down like a tablet.

"You can't even taste it," she said and pushed Oaf's glass toward her.

Oaf looked suspicious, but curious. She picked a pea off her plate, put it on her tongue, and swallowed it down quickly with a gulp of milk. "Mm," she said, nodding her head. She put another pea in her mouth and did it again. "My tablets."

Juliet lay in bed that night feeling heavy and tired. She'd heard of people feeling weighed down with worry and now she knew what they meant. Her limbs were so heavy she could barely pull up the covers. Her heart felt anchored to the bottom of the sea.

"Dimitri," she said, looking at the scruffy-tailed dog, "our family's in trouble." She told him all about her parents fighting and her sister refusing to eat her vegetables. "I managed to stop the fight this time, but who knows what'll happen next time?" She hung her worries on his branch and turned to the goat.

"Gwyneth," she said, "Nana had a fall last year, and I know you look after sickness and broken bones. Ever since she hurt herself, she's been cranky and sad, and she won't wear her safety alarm. I want to help her but I don't know how. Maybe you can help me come up with something."

Juliet stroked Gwyneth's horns, took her worries between her thumb and forefinger, and hung them on the tree. Feeling much lighter, she turned off her bedside light. "At least I don't have to worry about my friends," she said, laying her head on her pillow. "I don't, do I?"

It didn't take long for Juliet and Gemma to become good friends. Within two weeks, Juliet had invited her over to play at Gregson Street.

When the doorbell rang, Juliet was ready. She took one quick look around her bedroom to make sure it was perfect and went out to answer the door.

"Oh, my goodness," said Gemma, stepping into the hallway. "You've been burgled!"

"What? No, it's just my dad's research."

"Oh," said Gemma, sounding disappointed.

Juliet got the impression she would have found a burglary far more exciting.

"Come with me."

Gemma walked into Juliet's bedroom and

looked around carefully. Her eyes blinked rapidly, like a camera shutter, taking note of everything. Juliet watched with a vague sense of unease. Gemma seemed to absorb the life force out of everything she saw. It was as if each blink made the objects less Juliet's and more Gemma's.

"What's this?" said Gemma, striding over to the Worry Tree. She traced a finger along the ancient, bending branches, touching each of the animals. "Juliet?" she breathed. "Tell me about this tree. I want to know everything!"

Juliet suddenly felt shy about the Worry Tree. She didn't want to share its story or its secrets. She realized the tree was a part of her now, and to tell Gemma about it would be revealing too much of herself.

"Juliet?" prodded Gemma. "What's the story?" She flicked back her glossy nutmeg hair and smiled.

"Oh, um, we don't really know much about it. Here, come and look at some of my collections."

Gemma seemed drawn to the tree's quiet peacefulness, and Juliet had to cough twice to get her attention.

"Coming," said Gemma, though she moved very slowly.

Juliet opened a drawer, took out a box, and laid it on the yellowy green carpet. "See?" she said. "These are my erasers."

"Mm," said Gemma, looking over her shoulder at the Worry Tree. "Hey, what's that sound?"

"I dunno. Look," said Juliet, desperate to get her attention. "You can have one if you like."

Gemma turned around quickly. "Really? Can I?"

Juliet didn't particularly want to give away one of her erasers, but it was better than having to explain about the tree. "Come check them out."

She arranged the erasers on the floor in color groups: all the blue ones together, all the purple ones together, all the glittery ones together, and so on. Within each color, she laid them out in order of size, smallest to largest. Gemma soon spotted an eraser in the shape of a volcano.

"How cute is this!" she said and picked it up.

"That's the best one," said Juliet. "Dad gave it to me 'specially. It's from a volcano exhibition at the museum where he works."

Gemma turned the eraser over in her hand and examined it. It was made to split into two parts so you could see the hot lava core inside. Juliet liked to open it up and imagine real boiling lava pouring out the top.

"I love it," said Gemma. "I'll keep this one."

"Oh," said Juliet, "that's my favorite."

"No wonder," said Gemma. "It's great."

"Dad gave it to me *'specially,*" repeated Juliet.

"Mm," said Gemma. "So, can I have it?"

"What about this one?" said Juliet, holding up an eraser shaped like a star. She felt mean offering such a boring one, but she didn't want to give up the special eraser. Gemma picked up the star and turned it over.

"Mmm, nah," she said, putting it down. "I like the volcano one better. Oh, come on, Juliet. You'll let me have it, won't you?"

"Well . . . ," said Juliet, feeling worn down, "I guess you could borrow it." She watched with a pang as Gemma popped the volcano into the top pocket of her jacket, a satisfied smile on her lips.

"Why don't we feed Piranha?" said Juliet,

before Gemma could take anything else. "He's my Venus flytrap."

"Sure," said Gemma.

"I've got some flies here," said Juliet. "I—"

She broke off when she heard a strange scratching sound coming from nearby.

"Did you hear that?" she said.

"Yes," said Gemma. "What is it? A rat?"

Juliet looked over to where the sound was coming from. "Don't move, Gemma," she said. "I need to check something."

Juliet got up quickly and walked over to the wardrobe. She pulled on the handle and the door swung open. The girls gasped. Standing in the wardrobe, wearing a flashlight strapped to her head and holding a notepad and pen, was Oaf.

"Hi!" said Oaf. "What are you two up to? Can I join in?"

"What are *we* up to?" said Juliet. "What are *we* up to? What are *you* up to?"

"Nothing much," said Oaf, sliding the lid back on her pen. She flicked off the switch on her miner's light and stepped onto the carpet. "Can I play?"

"Oaf!" said Juliet, moving toward her.

"See ya!" said Oaf and dashed out of the room.

Juliet rolled her eyes. "You see what I have to put up with?"

Juliet lay in bed that night thinking of her volcano eraser. "Piers," she whispered to the peacock, looking at his proud face, "I've lost something, and I need you to look after it till morning." Piers looked happy to help. She hung her worries on his branch and turned to the dog.

"Dimitri," she said. "I've got Oaf trouble. You know what I mean." By the look on his face, she was sure Dimitri knew exactly what she meant. Juliet cupped the worry in her hand and gave it to him for safekeeping. Then she imagined climbing up the Worry Tree, escaping into its rustling cave of leaves, and falling asleep in the crook of a branch.

"The festival's coming up pretty soon," said Lindsay. "I'm going to bring along my axolotl and charge people for a hold."

"What's an axolotl?" said Gemma.

"Juliet," said Lindsay, turning her back on Gemma, "what are you going to bring?"

"What's an axolotl?" repeated Gemma.

Juliet looked from one friend to the other.

"It's kind of like an underwater lizard, Gemma," said Juliet, "and, Lindsay, I'm going to bring my plant collection: cacti, mostly, and maybe Piranha."

"Great," said Lindsay. "Be careful that Hugh doesn't take any of them."

"I don't have anything to bring," said Gemma.

"Don't you have any hobbies?" said Juliet.

"I like watching TV," said Gemma.

"Documentaries?" said Juliet. "I love documentaries, especially ones about nature and animals and things like that."

"I don't really like the programs," said Gemma. "I just watch the ads. Some of them are really good."

"Oh," said Juliet.

"How . . . educational," said Lindsay.

"Maybe I could sit with you at the festival, Juliet. Since I'm not bringing anything, I could help you mind your plants."

"Juliet's sitting next to me," said Lindsay. "Sorry."

"But won't you be sitting in the pet area?" said Gemma. "With your axywhatsit? That's in a different building from all the collections."

"It is," said Juliet. "Lindsay, we won't be able to sit together."

"What a shame," said Gemma, flashing her sugar-cube smile.

Lindsay scuffed her feet on the ground and said nothing.

"See you when I get home from work," said Mom as Juliet and Oaf climbed out of the car. "Sorry I can't stay. Make sure you visit your dad at the sausage sizzle stand."

It was the day of the festival, but Juliet had stopped looking forward to it a long time ago. Lindsay and Gemma were making life hard for her. It wasn't that they fought outright. It was more a polite, but deadly, tug of war.

Holding on to her box of plants, Juliet walked through the school gates. Oaf ran ahead of her, heading straight for the dunking machine. There were people everywhere, setting up stalls with cakes and toilet-paper holders and bags of potpourri. Juliet walked past the ring toss and the raffle and made her way into the classroom.

"Hey, Jooly-Wooly. What dumb hobby did you bring along?"

Hugh. Just what Juliet needed. She set her box on the table and took out a sign she'd made the night before. Written on cardboard in thick brown marker were her initials: JJJ, just like three upside-down walking sticks in a row.

"Joooooly," said Hugh. "Joooooly, why won't you talk to me?"

Juliet ignored him. When all the cacti were in place, she carefully lifted out her prized possession: Piranha. She didn't take him out very often, but today was a special occasion. He might help her win the prize for most unusual collection.

"What's that?" said Hugh, crossing the floor. "A man-eating plant? Great!" And he popped a Smartie into one of Piranha's traps.

"Don't!" said Juliet. "You'll kill him." But she was already too late. Piranha had closed his trap.

Hugh smirked. "Looks like he was hungry," he said and tipped another Smartie into his hand. "I think he wants another one."

"Hugh—"

73

He was about to drop it into a different trap when Mr. Castelli came into the room.

"Hello, kids. What's this then? Looks like we've got a couple of contenders for most unusual collection. A Venus flytrap from Juliet, and, Hugh, I see you've brought a jar of your own bellybutton lint. Wonderful, wonderful." Mr. Castelli tugged on his hairy ear and smiled. "Good luck, kids. I'll be round and about, so give me a holler if you need anything. Make sure to come and try my homemade sushi at the Japanese food stall."

Gemma arrived soon after, and Hugh very quickly went back to his side of the classroom. Piranha, who obviously didn't like Smarties, opened his trap once more. Juliet picked out the Smartie and threw it away. Now things were looking up.

And I haven't bitten my nails once, thought Juliet.

Then Lindsay came to visit.

"Ready?" she said, sitting on the edge of the desk.

"Yep," said Juliet.

"What's happening?" said Gemma. "Are we going someplace?"

"Juliet and I are going to walk around and visit her dad at the sausage sizzle," said Lindsay.

"Yes," said Juliet, then noticed the hurt look in Gemma's eyes. "You can come too, if you like."

"That won't work," said Lindsay quickly. "I mean, who's going to look after your plants?"

"Oh, yeah," said Juliet. "I forgot. Maybe I should stay back and you two go."

"No!" said Lindsay and Gemma together.

"Gemma doesn't mind looking after your plants, do you, Gemma?" said Lindsay. "We don't want Hugh touching them."

Gemma glared at Lindsay but smiled at Juliet. "Anything for my best friend," she said.

Lindsay glared back at Gemma, then seized hold of Juliet's arm.

"We'll bring you a hot dog," said Juliet as Lindsay dragged her out the door. "Won't be long!"

The festival was a whirl of silly games, sticky toffee, bouncer castles, and the smell of sausages. In spite of herself, Juliet began to enjoy the day.

She and Lindsay had a good look around, then bought three hot dogs. Later, they went back to Gemma to pack up before the awards ceremony.

Everyone gathered on the oval in front of Mr. Castelli. He stood behind a podium tapping his microphone.

"Ladies and gentlemen, parents, students, pets, if I may have your attention, please. It's time for the awards ceremony to begin."

Juliet stood between her two friends, Piranha in her arms. Lindsay was holding on to a goldfish bowl with her axolotl pressing its nose up against the glass. Gemma was guarding the box of cactus plants. Juliet patted Piranha for reassurance and took a deep breath. I hope I win, I hope I win, I hope I win, she thought.

"I heard Hugh bullied a lot of the little kids into voting for him," said Lindsay.

"Really?" said Juliet. "He's such a—ouch!" She felt a stinging sensation on the back of her head. "What was that?"

Juliet turned around to see what had made her head sting. Hugh was standing behind her, holding a hair he had just pulled out of her head.

"Just making sure it's real," he said, lifting it up to the sun and peering at it. "Not drawn on or anything."

"Just ignore him," whispered Lindsay.

Hugh reached over to pull out another hair.

"Don't," said Juliet, "or I'll pull your hair!" Juliet smiled to herself. She'd talked back to him at last.

"I'm wearing a cap, dumbo. You can't touch my hair."

"Oh," said Juliet. "Well, maybe I'll, um, maybe I'll, ah, what I mean is—"

"She meant your nose hair," said Gemma. "Touch her again and she'll yank out your nose hair. Or I will."

Gemma moved toward him, holding up her thumb and forefinger. Hugh backed away quickly.

"Thanks," said Juliet. She was pleased to have Gemma on her side, though sorry she needed someone to come to her rescue again.

"Shh," said Lindsay, "Mr. Castelli's opening the envelope for your award, Juliet."

"All the votes have been counted," said their teacher, "and I'm pleased to announce the winner of the Students' Choice Award for most unusual collection is . . . Hugh Allen, for his jar of belly-button lint! Hugh, could you make your way up to the podium, please?"

"Hugh!" snorted Lindsay.

"Unbelievable!" said Gemma.

"There must be some mistake," said Juliet. She hugged Piranha close to her chest.

"There's no mistake," said Hugh, pushing past. "I'm just superior, that's all. As if anyone would ever vote for you."

Juliet dropped her eyes. He'd won again. Piranha looked upset, so she took her box of cacti from Gemma and put him inside. That way, he wouldn't have to witness Hugh waving his trophy in the air and yelling, "I'm a legend! I'm the champion! I'm the most superior human being in the world!"

"Don't worry, Juliet," said Lindsay. "You can come over to my place now and we'll work on my fish pond. You'll forget all about him."

"Or," said Gemma, "you could come to my place and we'll plot our revenge."

"I invited her first," said Lindsay.

"But she'll have more fun with me," said Gemma.

"I'm a bit busy today," said Juliet. "I'm not sure I can go to anyone's place."

"But, Juliet!" said Lindsay and Gemma.

As Juliet looked from one friend to the other, Dad came up from behind.

"Better luck next time, hey, kiddo?"

"I suppose so," said Juliet. "Can we find Oaf and go home now? Like, immediately."

"Sure thing. But before we do, I have some news I hope will cheer you up. You too, Gemma and Lindsay. That Hugh character may have won that award but I won four free tickets to the movies on the ring toss. Why don't I take you three girls out next weekend to make up for all this? What do you say?"

Juliet watched her friends closely.

"Sure, Mr. Jones," said Gemma, glancing at Lindsay.

"That'd be great," said Lindsay, glancing back at Gemma.

This'll be interesting, thought Juliet.

Juliet lay in bed that night thinking of her friends.

"Wolfgang," she said, "they're driving me crazy! Do wombats have this kind of trouble as well? What is wrong with Lindsay, anyway? She's been mean to Gemma from the very start. I wish I could make them be nice to each other. Maybe spending time together at the movies will give them each a chance to see how great the

other one is. That might work . .
might. Wish me luck for the rest o
Wolfgang. And thanks for every
know what to do."

"Dad."

"Yes, kiddo?"

"Do you promise not to talk to strangers when
we get to the cinema?"

Dad smiled. "I thought kids only got embarrassed by their parents once they hit puberty."

"Dad!" said Juliet. "And promise you won't
use the word *puberty*."

The cinema lobby was crowded with people
but it didn't take long for Juliet to spot Lindsay
and Gemma. They were sitting over in a corner
with their heads bent together, writing on a
sheet of paper.

When Lindsay spotted them, she folded the
sheet in half and put it behind her back. Gemma
smiled. Dad shook their hands heartily and bel-
lowed hello, and Juliet waved her hand, fresh
Band-Aids plastered on every finger.

"Here, girls," said Dad, plunging his arm into his army supply backpack. "Have some M&M's. I picked them up at the supermarket this morning."

Juliet looked horrified. "Dad! You don't eat supermarket stuff at the movies. We need proper M&M's! From the snack bar."

"But aren't supermarket M&M's exactly the same as cinema M&M's?" said Dad. "Apart from being much cheaper."

For the sake of their friend, Gemma and Lindsay pretended not to notice. Juliet shook her head.

"I guess you girls won't be interested in any homemade popcorn, then?" said Dad, pulling out a large red Tupperware container. "I made it myself!"

Dad left for the ticket booth, and Juliet sat down by her friends.

"We've got something for you," said Lindsay, pulling the sheet of paper out from behind her back. "We think you'll find it interesting."

"A quiz?" said Juliet. "You've made me a quiz? Great!" Juliet hoped she got the answers right.

"All you have to do is answer three questions," said Lindsay.

"Go for it," said Juliet. "I'm ready."

"Question number one," said Lindsay, pushing her wiry hair out of her eyes, "would you rather be very rich or very famous?"

Juliet scrunched up her forehead in thought. "I reckon . . . famous," she said. "Yep, famous. Maybe for making an amazing scientific discovery or something."

Lindsay smirked at Gemma, a gleam of triumph in her eyes. Gemma grabbed the paper from her and took Juliet's hand.

"The second question's far more important," she said, "so listen carefully. Would you rather be able to breathe underwater or fly through the air?"

Juliet felt uncomfortable now. Gemma was gripping her hand awfully tight. Something was up, but she wasn't sure what it was.

"Breathe underwater, I guess," she replied.

It was Gemma's turn to smile in triumph. Lindsay shot her a look of fury.

"Give it back," said Lindsay. "There's still one question to go."

Juliet suddenly realized what was going on. Each question had two options: one was Gemma's answer, one was Lindsay's. This quiz wasn't a quiz at all. It was a test to see who should be Juliet's best friend.

"Juliet?" said Lindsay. "Are you ready for the last question?"

"Not really," said Juliet.

"Number three, would you rather lose your sense of taste or lose your sense of smell?"

Juliet felt trapped. Whichever answer she

chose, one of her friends would be angry. She looked from one friend to the other. Lindsay, her oldest, most wiry-haired friend, wore a pained but hopeful expression. Gemma, her newest and bravest friend, flashed her sugar-cube smile. Juliet's insides churned. "Ah," she said. "Um . . . what's the question again?"

"Would you rather lose your sense of taste or lose your sense of smell?"

"Actually," said Dad, arriving back from the ticket booth, "if you lose your sense of smell, you automatically lose your sense of taste. Not entirely, of course. You can sometimes tell the difference between sweet and sour tastes, but when it comes to telling the difference between, say, a Granny Smith and a Jonathan apple, you're in a bit of trouble. You may be interested to know that people born without a sense of smell suffer from a medical condition called congenital anosmia. . . ."

Saved! Juliet had never been more glad of Dad's scientific facts. Lindsay and Gemma exchanged irritated glances, and Lindsay screwed the quiz into a ball and threw it into a nearby bin.

So, thought Juliet, the quiz is history, thanks to Dad. The question remains: what will they think of next?

After Juliet had checked in the wardrobe and under her bed and was satisfied Oaf wasn't hiding anywhere, she lay down on the carpet for a worm's eye view of the Worry Tree.

"Wolfgang," she began, "you would not believe what happened at the movies today!" And she filled him in on the awful events. Wolfgang's eyes twinkled, inviting her to hang her worries on his branch for the night. She got up on her knees and handed them over. He seemed to be saying, "Let me help. You need a break tonight. You have enough to worry about during the day." Juliet knew this was true. School worries would just have to wait. Now it was time for sleep.

It was Sunday, the day after the movies, so Juliet had one whole day to herself before school started again. She decided to spend the afternoon sorting her collections. By six o'clock, she was ready to relax in front of the television.

When she walked into the living room, Oaf was sitting in a beanbag chair.

"Juliet," she said. "I can't find the remote."

While Juliet felt behind the sofa cushions, Mom came into the room.

"Dinner's almost ready," she said, leaning on the doorframe. "Juliet, could you set the table, please? I'm dishing up in a minute."

"It's not my turn tonight," said Juliet. "It's Oaf's."

"Fine," sighed Mom. "Whatever." She walked back down the hall toward the kitchen.

Oaf slid lower in her beanbag, just like a sunken soufflé.

"You'd better go set the table," said Juliet. "I think Mom's in a bad mood."

"Mom asked you," said Oaf.

"Oaf, it's not my turn."

"But Mom asked you."

"But it's your turn."

"But Mom asked you."

"Oaf! That's because she didn't realize I'd set the table yesterday. You're the one who should do it."

"Mmm," said Oaf, pretending to think. "I don't think so."

Juliet pursed her lips like a drawstring bag. Normally, she'd be happy to help out Mom, just to be nice, but Juliet was now in a bad mood herself. What's more, this was a matter of principle. Oaf never did any work around the house, and Juliet was tired of picking up the slack. Now was probably not the best time to take a stand, but that was just too bad. Juliet stayed in her chair and watched TV too.

Five minutes passed, then Mom's tired voice funneled down the hallway. "Kids! I see the table, but it doesn't look set!"

Juliet wondered if it was possible, by sheer force of will, to pass on a sense of responsibility from one person (Juliet) to another person (Oaf). After several minutes of intense concentration, she realized the answer was no.

Juliet heard Mom's footsteps in the corridor, followed by the sound of boxes being shoved about. Mom poked her head into the living room looking an odd shade of purple. Eggplant purple, thought Juliet. Mom was the kind of person who spent her days a cheerful, rosy pink. Juliet didn't like to see her purple. When your mother's face is purple, you want to be careful.

"Girls," said Mom slowly and quietly, "you have one minute to set the table."

"But, Mom," said Juliet, "it's Oaf's turn to do it. She's the one you should be asking."

"No, it's not," said Oaf.

"I—really—do—not—care—whose—turn—it—is—so—long—as—it—is—done!" said Mom.

"But—"

"One minute!" snapped Mom. "And one minute only, or there'll be hell to pay. Hell—to—pay."

"I wonder how much hell costs," muttered Oaf. "It might be as much as two hundred dollars. I hope I don't have to pay for it out of my allowance."

Juliet rolled her eyes.

One minute passed. Then two. It was time to go eat.

Juliet sat quietly at the dinner table feeling guilty. Neither she nor Oaf had set the table. It's a Matter of Principle, she thought. Mom should have made Oaf set the table, not the good and trustworthy daughter! It's a Matter of Principle, a Matter of Principle.

Dad stirred in the bedroom, then came out and joined them.

A Matter of Principle, a Matter of Principle.

Mom clanked pots and pans in the kitchen.

A Matter of Principle, a Matter of Principle.

Nana shuffled into the room and sat down.

A Matter of Principle, a Matter of Principle.

Oaf sang softly under her breath.

A Matter of Principle, a Matter of Principle, a Pratter of Minciple, a Pattle of Minciter. . . .

What would Mom say?

As it turned out, Mom said nothing at all. She just stood in the doorway of the dining room, holding a pot of spaghetti in one hand and a ladle in the other. The silence was terrible. It was a thick, stifling, pillow-over-the-face kind of silence. Even Oaf, who had the nerves of a knife-thrower's assistant, fidgeted.

Mom stepped forward, lifted up the ladle, and served five piles of the spaghetti straight onto the tabletop, one in front of each person. They looked like five upturned buckets of worms, oozing and slithering about. Mom went back into the kitchen and returned with another pot. This one contained the bolognese sauce. Juliet watched in horror as Mom dumped minced meat and tomatoes right on top of the spaghetti.

"Interesting," said Dad, nodding his head, "but perfectly hygienic. In some parts of India, people don't use cutlery at all. They—"

"Martin!" said Mom. "Can we just eat?"

Dad closed his mouth.

"Mom," said Juliet, once Mom had sat down, "we . . . we haven't got any forks to eat with."

"Right!" said Mom, "*I'll* get them then, shall I, since no one else in this family does any work around here?" She stormed out of the room and came back with five forks. "Anything else, people? Drinks, perhaps?"

The rest of them shook their heads, horrified at the thought of what Mom might do with a bottle of orange juice and no glasses.

"So, Nana," said Dad, trying to lighten the mood, "tell us what you got up to in craft class today."

"Craft class?" said Nana slowly. "What did I do in craft class today?"

Juliet didn't like the tone of her voice. She sounded . . . fed up.

"In craft class," she went on, "I spent three hours decorating my TV remote control with seashells and glass beads, so I'm pleased to report my Ph.D. in biochemistry hasn't gone to waste."

"Oh," said Juliet, feeling anxious.

"Let's just say it goes well with the self-portrait I did the other day, the one made out of dried macaroni."

"If you don't like that craft class, maybe we could find you another one," said Mom, "or perhaps some other activity."

"Oh?" said Nana. "Like bingo, you mean? Or I could join the Seniors Who Knit Club, and we could all sit around and discuss doilies. Or maybe I could join the I've Got Ingrown Toenails and Want to Complain About My Feet Society. I hear they're looking for members."

"Are they?" said Oaf, peeling off her sock.

"Oaf!" said Mom. "No bare feet at the table."

Oaf sighed and put her sock back on. Nana huffed and Juliet frowned.

"Righto, then," said Dad heartily. "Guess what I found today! My old chemistry set. I thought I could set it up again and do some experiments."

Oaf turned to Dad with shining eyes. "Can we make explosions?" she said.

"Possibly, possibly," said Dad.

"I guess that means you've been mucking around rather than clearing that junk out of the hallway," said Mom. She was looking purple again, and Juliet didn't like it. Words like *divorce*, *custody battle*, and *hostage situation* popped into her mind.

"Well, Martin?" said Mom. "Did you get any work done on the boxes? The boxes in the hall I was lucky enough to stub my toe on this evening?"

"Oh . . . ah . . . well . . . ," said Dad.

"Typical!" said Mom. "You didn't even try!"

"Karen, that's completely unfair! You're just in a bad mood, and you're taking it out on me."

"Oh, I'm in a bad mood, am I? And who, pray tell, put me in this bad mood?"

Juliet hated it when adults asked angry questions they already knew the answers to.

"Our hall looks like a dump site," said Mom. "I'd like to invite some people over, but how can I? Couldn't you at least try?"

Juliet shut her ears. She was feeling sick, and her skin was all prickly. Lindsay had once told her you could only keep seven thoughts in your head at any one time. Juliet tried to think of seven things to help her forget about the fight. Why are eggs egg-shaped? she thought desperately. Why is yawning contagious? How many planets are there in the solar system? How many moons does each planet have and what are their names?

But it was no use. Mom and Dad were too loud.

"Well!" said Nana. "So much for harmony on Gregson Street."

"You needn't criticize," said Dad. "Look at you! You're not wearing your safety alarm. Again! What if you fell over and no one was there to help?"

"Don't speak to me that way, Martin! I'm a grown woman, I'll have you know."

Then Oaf began humming.

"Ophelia!" said Mom. "Give it a rest, will you? You're in no position to be causing trouble tonight, young lady. I mean it!"

Juliet wanted to do something to save the situation. Anything. Then she had an idea. "Wait!" she cried with a kind of desperate brightness. "Why don't we all Name Our Feelings?"

Everyone stopped talking, looked at Juliet, and then, just as quickly, went back to their arguing.

It seemed to Juliet as though a war had broken out. Mom was mad at Dad because Dad had made the house look like a dump site. Dad was mad at Mom for getting angry with him for making the house look like a dump site. The house looked like a dump site because all the boxes, which used to live in Juliet's room, now had nowhere to live. So if Juliet had never got her own room, Dad would still have his study. Then there wouldn't be any stuff in the hall, the place wouldn't look like a dump site, and Dad and Mom wouldn't be fighting. So really, the whole thing was her fault! Juliet felt utterly miserable.

As the voices rose around her, the glimmer of an idea flashed through her mind. It was an idea that made her sad, but she knew it would solve all their problems. "Stop!" she cried, getting to her feet. "Everybody stop! This is all my fault, but I know how to fix it!"

Juliet looked around the room at Mom, Dad, Nana, and Oaf. She sighed a great and noble sigh. "I'm going to give up my room," she said. "Dad can have the study back, and everything will be the way it's always been, okay? No more fighting. It's all going to be fixed."

Everyone stared back in stunned silence. A little sob escaped from Juliet's lips, and she ran out of the room.

Juliet lay in her own bed in the room that would soon become Dad's study once more. She thought about Life and wondered why it was always such hard work. Why couldn't people just be nice to each other once in a while? She felt awful about losing her room, awful about the fighting, awful about Nana being cranky, and awful about her friends. There were so many things to feel awful about, she didn't know where to begin. Even when she'd gone through each worry, she still felt bad. It was as though she was still carrying a problem, but she didn't know what it was. All she knew was that it was really heavy and it hurt a lot.

She looked at the photograph of Nana on her bedside table. Nana had said if ever there was a problem too hard to describe, she should put it in the hollow in the trunk of the Worry Tree. Juliet wished she could crawl into that hole and never come out. She reached up and touched the inky black spot. She felt her worries trickle down her arm, to her fingertips and into the hollow of the tree. "Time for sleep," she said wearily and switched off the light.

Juliet didn't feel like talking to anyone the next morning so she ate her breakfast alone on the veranda. On the walk to school, Oaf grumbled about having to share her room again.

"Where am I supposed to keep my maggot farm now?"

Juliet ignored Oaf, her mind on other things: specifically, what had Gemma and Lindsay cooked up for her today?

She didn't have to wait long to find out.

"So," said Lindsay, as the three girls opened their lunch boxes, "did you see the list that's going around?"

"What list?" said Juliet warily.

"It's the one where you write down the name of everyone in the class, then put a number next to their name," said Lindsay.

"They used to do it at my old school," said Gemma. "You're meant to number everyone in class from the person you like the best to the person you like the worst."

"But the most important thing," said Lindsay, "is to put your *best* friend first."

Oh, thought Juliet. So that's what they're up to.

"Here," said Gemma, "I've got some pens."

"And I've got some paper," said Lindsay. "I've already written everyone's name down, so all you have to do is number them."

Lindsay and Gemma bent over their papers and started scribbling. Juliet rubbed her eyes, exhausted. How was she going to get out of this one? She wanted to cry or scream or bite her nails or *something*. No matter what she did, her friends were going to make her choose. But how could she? She liked them both—Lindsay for her brains and her curiosity and the fact that they'd been friends ever since kindergarten, and Gemma because she was funny and brave.

There were also things she didn't like about the two of them, like Lindsay's dark moods and the way she was unfriendly to new people. Or the way Gemma grabbed things without thinking (like that volcano eraser). How on earth could she choose between them? Whatever she decided, she'd end up losing a friend.

"Juliet?" said Gemma. "Are you done yet?"

"Yeah," said Lindsay. "Hurry up."

The V-shaped crease appeared between Juliet's eyebrows, and her rash crept slowly up her arms. If they wanted an answer so badly, well, she'd give them one. She just hoped they were prepared for the outcome.

"I'm done," said Juliet, pressing her list to her chest.

"Well, come on," said Gemma. "Let's see it."

"Pass me yours first," said Juliet. "You too, Lindsay."

The girls shrugged and handed over their lists. Juliet took them, weighed them in her hands, and ripped them in two and then two again.

"Hey!" said Lindsay. "Aren't you going to even look at them?"

"I don't need to," said Juliet. "I know you put me first, and I know Gemma did too."

"True," said Gemma, "but what we really want to know is, who did *you* put first?"

"Yes," said Lindsay. "Who do you like best?"

Juliet felt anger boiling up from her toes like

milk on the stove. Any second now, it would overflow.

"Come on, Juliet," said Lindsay. "It's unfair to make us wait."

"Yeah," said Gemma. "Don't be mean."

"What?" said Juliet, slowly, dangerously. "Did you just call me mean and unfair?"

Lindsay and Gemma swapped anxious glances. Juliet's face was purple.

"Jul—"

"How dare you say that about me! *What is wrong with you two?* I am absolutely, completely, and utterly sick of you two and the way you keep fighting over me! Does it really matter who I put first on this piece of paper? Really?"

Gemma and Lindsay looked down.

"If you really want to know who I put as number one, you'll just have to read my list, which"—and she snatched it away before the two girls could touch it—"which I'll give to you in a minute. But I want you to know something first. I have been miserable for weeks because of you two. Totally miserable. All this trying to make me choose and stuff has been awful, and I've had enough! So read my list and remember, this decision is final. I will never talk about it again, and if either of you tries to bring it up, I'll just sit by myself at lunch! At least then I'd get some peace!"

At this, Juliet threw her list on the ground and stormed across the playground. Lindsay and Gemma looked at each other, then at the paper. They both bent down to pick it up, but Gemma was quicker.

"Well?" said Lindsay. "C'mon, what's it say?"

Gemma took her time smoothing out the paper, then held it close to her chest so Lindsay couldn't see. "Wow," she said, flashing her sugar-cube smile. "I don't believe it! I'm number one! That means Juliet likes me best!"

"What?!" said Lindsay. "There is no way! *I'm* her oldest friend! Here, give it to me!" She snatched the list away from Gemma to check for herself. "What? . . . That doesn't make sense. Oh . . . I see what she's done. Look, Gemma, you made a mistake. You're not the only one who's number one. She's gone and picked us both!"

Juliet sat on a wooden bench and ate her yogurt with great ferocity. When she spotted Lindsay and Gemma walking toward her, she decided to say nothing. If they were angry with her, that was just too bad.

"Is it okay if we sit here?" said Lindsay.

"If you don't mind," said Gemma.

Juliet nodded curtly.

The two girls took their seats, one on each side of her. There was an awkward silence, but Juliet didn't care. She just kept eating her yogurt.

Lindsay finally spoke. "Juliet," she said, "I was going to go buy some stuff to make a sandwich in a minute. Would you like a bite if I did? Gemma, you can have some too, if you want."

Juliet put down her spoon. She'd thought Lindsay was going to tell her off. Instead, she was asking her to share a sandwich. Juliet knew this was Lindsay's way of saying, "I'm sorry."

"All right," said Juliet, smiling with relief. "Sounds good."

Lindsay smiled back, knowing this was Juliet's way of saying, "I forgive you."

A moment later, Gemma opened the zipper of her top pocket and took something out. "I thought you might like this back," she said.

"My volcano eraser!" said Juliet. "Thanks!"

Juliet turned it over in her hands. She was shocked her outburst had produced such good results.

"There's something else too," said Gemma. "I was wondering if you and Lindsay would like to come over and play at my house sometime. We've got a big TV, and we could watch some shows. Even nature documentaries, if you like. But only if you want to."

Juliet grinned. She felt like singing. "What do you think, Lindsay?"

Lindsay didn't look overjoyed, but she nodded yes, and Juliet knew she would try her best to be nice.

Well, thought Juliet, that's one problem down. Bring on the next one!

The walk home from school was Juliet's happiest in a long while. Lindsay and Gemma were making an effort, and she hadn't heard a peep out of Hugh in ages.

Unfortunately, Juliet's good mood dried up the moment she got home and stepped into her bedroom. The Worry Tree animals seemed to be looking at her with great sadness in their eyes. It was as though they knew she'd promised to give them up.

"I'm sorry," said Juliet, touching each of them in turn. "But it was the only way I could think of to save my family."

Needing a chocolate milk to cheer herself up, she left her room and headed for the kitchen. She was almost there when she heard muttering coming from inside. As she opened the door, Mom and Dad sprang apart.

"Oh, hello, love," said Mom. "We were just discussing . . ."

"Weedkiller!" said Dad.

"Yes, that's right," said Mom. "Weedkiller. We, um . . ."

"Don't like them," said Dad. "Weeds, that is."

"No, no, can't stand them," said Mom. "Dreadful things. Dreadful."

"Dreadful," added Dad.

Juliet looked from Dad to Mom and back again. They were certainly acting very strangely.

It was with a heavy heart that Juliet went to her bedroom that night. Not only was she losing her Worry Tree, her parents seemed to be cracking up.

"I guess I'll start packing tomorrow," she said to the animals. "That means this will be my last night with you. Dimitri, Wolfgang, Delia, Petronella, Gwyneth, Piers—you've all been such great friends to me these past few weeks.

I don't know what I'd have done without you. Thanks so much."

Juliet kissed the tips of her fingers, then pressed them on the nose or beak of each animal.

"Good night," she said sadly, and switched off the light.

It was three o'clock in the morning and Juliet needed to go to the bathroom. She felt around in the dark for her flashlight. Written on the handle in thick gold marker were her initials: JJJ, just like three saxophones in a row.

She got up and padded down the hallway. Before she got to the bathroom, she noticed a strange orange glow coming through the window, flickering like firelight. Juliet pulled back the curtain to have a better look. It *was* firelight! Down by the barbecue area. Someone was out there too. Someone in a frilly nightie. Someone who looked like Nana.

Juliet opened the back door slowly and crept out onto the veranda. The concrete felt cool under her feet. Smoke curled upward into the night sky as Nana poked the fire with a large pair of tongs. Juliet came closer. In among the flames was a heap of cork animals and paper doilies, gradually turning black. On the ground was a pile of Nana's craft projects: Popsicle-stick photo frames, pipe cleaners with googly eyes, egg cartons, macramé pot holders—all waiting to be burned. Nana picked up a handful and tossed them into the fire.

"Hello, Nana," said Juliet slowly. "What are you doing?"

"Juliet," said Nana, "I've had enough! There comes a point in a woman's life when you have to say no. No more doilies! No more dried macaroni! No more making things that clutter up the living room! Basically, what I'm saying is *No!*"

She plunged her tongs into the fire, and sparks flew up into the air like confetti. Juliet nodded. Nana obviously needed someone to talk to, and, since there was no one else around, it would have to be her.

"Nana," she said, "I've noticed you've been kind of—"

"Cranky?" said Nana. "Ill-tempered? Cross? Tetchy?"

"Yeah," said Juliet. "Why?"

Nana sighed and the collar of her nightie fluttered up, making her look like a frill-necked lizard.

"It's a lot of things, Juliet," said Nana, tossing another load of pipe cleaners onto the fire. "A lot of things. This, for one," she said, holding up her safety alarm. "I'd love to throw this in the fire."

"Nana! No!"

"Don't worry. I'm not going to. It's just that I absolutely hate wearing it."

"Why?" said Juliet. "It could save your life."

"That's true, but the moment I put this on, I'm admitting I'm old, O–L–D, old. There's no turning back then. I'm basically saying I can't manage on my own, and that makes me feel useless. Look at me. I used to be head of the university's chemistry department and now all I seem to do is sit around and make knickknacks out of clothespins and corks."

"So that's why you're burning them," said Juliet.

"That's why I'm burning them," said Nana. "I've turned a corner, Juliet. It's time for a change. I'm just not sure what that change will be."

Juliet looked thoughtful. It sounded as though Nana had a lot on her mind. No wonder she'd been so cranky. "Maybe I could tell Delia about your worries," said Juliet. At least for tonight, she added silently. "She could look after them for you."

"Delia, the duck?" said Nana. "Of course! Getting used to change is her job. Thank you, Juliet. I would very much appreciate that."

Juliet looked into the flames and smiled. To be useful, she thought, is the best feeling in the world.

Juliet awoke to the sound of scraping noises coming from Oaf's room. She groaned loudly and turned over to look at the Worry Tree animals. They looked pretty tired, and no wonder: she'd given them a lot of work to do lately.

There was a light tapping at the door and then a creak. Mom and Dad, still in their pajamas, stood in the doorway smiling.

"Can we come in for a sec, kiddo?" said Dad.

Juliet nodded, propping herself up on her elbows. No doubt they wanted to make arrangements for the big move back into Oaf's room.

"Your father and I have been talking," said Mom.

"What about?" said Juliet. "Not weedkiller again."

"No, no, not weedkiller," said Mom. "We weren't actually talking about that yesterday. The truth is, we were talking about you. We were quite shocked when you offered to give up your room on Sunday night."

"Very shocked," said Dad.

"I didn't know how else to fix things," said Juliet.

"That's just it," said Mom. "The fact that you thought it was up to you to fix everything."

"Your mother and I are quite ashamed," said Dad. "Ashamed that you would blame yourself for something that wasn't your fault. The fact is, our fights have nothing to do with you."

"But how can it not be my fault?" said Juliet. "Those boxes wouldn't be in the hall if it weren't for me."

"We always planned for you and Oaf to have your own rooms one day," said Mom. "The real issue is how we went about it."

"So what does that mean?" said Juliet.

"It means," said Dad, "that some things are *your* problem, and some things are *our* problem, and this thing happens to be *our* problem. And what that means is that we have to sort it out, not you."

"Dad and I have come to a decision," said Mom. "We're going to build a shed in the back-yard to store your dad's 'research.'"

"A big shed!" said Dad.

"A small shed," said Mom.

"At any rate," said Dad, "you don't have to move back in with your sister."

Juliet laughed. "That's great!"

A loud bang came from Oaf's room.

"What was that?" said Mom.

"Oaf," said Juliet. "I think she's barricading herself into her bedroom."

"Then we'd better go give her the good news," said Dad. "Quickly."

Mom and Dad kissed Juliet on the forehead and left. She flopped back down on her pillow and smiled with relief. She'd never thought of things *not* being her problem. She generally thought everything was her problem, even if she hadn't caused it. The Worry Tree animals looked at her as if they'd known all along and were glad she'd finally figured it out. Like warm water running into a cold bath, a sense of understanding spread throughout her body. Her arms relaxed, her legs relaxed, her mind relaxed, her heart felt free.

Not everything is my problem, she thought. And even better, I get to keep my room!

"Oaf!" called Juliet. "Have you seen my Band-Aids? I can't find them."

"There's none left," said Oaf. "I had to plug the leaks in our life raft."

"We don't have a life raft," said Juliet cautiously.

"We do now," said Oaf. "I made one out of plastic bags and a cooler."

Juliet gritted her teeth and pushed down a scream. Putting on her Band-Aids was part of her routine. What would happen if she changed it? She looked at the friendly faces of the Worry Tree animals. They seemed to be cheering her on, reminding her that she was "a capable person who could handle any crisis," just like the plaque on her wall said.

"I can do this," she said to herself and waggled her fingers in the air. She threw on her backpack and went into the hallway. "Come on, Oaf! It's time for school!"

Things couldn't have been better. Juliet's parents had stopped fighting, she didn't have to give up her Worry Tree animals, and, she was pleased to note, Gemma and Lindsay were actually sharing a bag of chips. Juliet stood up and stretched her legs, enjoying the sun on her face. Today was a Good Day, she thought.

At that moment, a small, wet object stung her on the arm.

"Hey!" she said and looked around to see where it had come from.

Gemma and Lindsay looked too.

"Over there," said Lindsay. "See?"

Peeping around the corner was Hugh, a pen tube held between his lips. He fired another spitball and ducked around the corner. Juliet's happy mood faded away to nothing. "Why now?" she said. "Why?"

"Don't worry," said Gemma, "I'll sort him out." She reached into her pocket for her Xtreme Sportz Bettina.

"You know what?" said Lindsay, getting to her feet. "I got Martial Artz Bettina and Hired Assazzin Bettina for my birthday. They're in my bag. With the two of us working together, Gemma, Hugh won't dare bother Juliet."

"Go, Lindsay!" said Gemma.

"Actually," said Juliet, looking at her friends, "three people working together would be even better. Pass me that Bettina, Lindsay. I'm coming too."

So there they stood, shoulder to shoulder, feet apart, eyes flashing, and the next time Hugh poked his head around the corner, there were three girls charging toward him, brandishing dolls in their hands.

Juliet and Dad stood outside a shop painted with large Japanese characters.

"Are you sure this is what you want to get?" asked Dad.

"Yep," said Juliet. "I've been thinking about it for a long time, and I reckon it's just what she needs."

"Okay," said Dad. "It's unusual, but you know your Nana better than anyone."

Juliet nodded. Once you've stood around a bonfire in the middle of the night burning paper doilies and talking about Life, you get to know someone pretty well.

When they got back to 23 Gregson Street, Nana's birthday party began.

"Open mine! Open mine!" said Oaf.

Nana took Oaf's present with an air of great respect and lifted the lid. "Goodness!" she said. "How . . . extraordinary." She held the box out so everyone could see. Inside was a lumpy purple blob the size of a mandarin orange.

"It's chewed-up bubblegum," said Oaf. "I made the Wattle Street record: nineteen pieces *and* a Mars Bar. Don't worry about it going bad, though. I varnished it with lacquer!"

"Innovative," said Dad.

"Interesting," said Mom.

"Typical," said Juliet.

"But heartfelt," said Nana. "Thank you, Oaf. I'll keep it by my bedside."

"Now me," said Juliet and she went over to the cupboard to get her present.

"While Juliet's doing that," said Nana, "I've got an announcement to make: I've officially given up craft class."

"Have you?" said Mom.

"I have. I realized if I went to one more session, I'd end up doing something very unpleasant with all that dried macaroni. I've decided to take up computing instead."

"You're going to learn computing!" said Dad. "That's fantastic!"

"No, Martin," said Nana patiently. "I'm not going to learn computing; I'm going to teach computing."

"Really?" said Dad.

"Don't sound so surprised," said Nana. "I've arranged it with University of the Third Age."

"Good for you!" said Mom.

"That's great!" said Juliet and Oaf.

"I had no idea," said Dad, "but it's brilliant news."

It was time for Juliet's present, so she handed it over and Nana opened the card. Written at the bottom in thick black marker were Juliet's initials: JJJ, just like three umbrella handles in a row. Nana unwrapped the present and balanced it on her lap. It was a small black pot containing a tiny tree with tiny branches and leaves.

"It's a Japanese bonsai tree," said Juliet.

"I've heard of them."

"Mr. Castelli says Japanese people spend ages and ages imagining what their tree's going to look like. Then they trim the branches with tiny hedge clippers until it looks exactly like the tree in their imagination."

"It's absolutely beautiful," said Nana, turning it around so she could see it from every angle. "Magical."

"There's something else," said Juliet, leaning in close so only Nana could hear. "It's actually a Worry Tree. I know you haven't had a tree in your bedroom for a very long time, so I bought you one."

Nana's eyes shone with tears. "What a wonderful idea!" she said. "This is exactly what I need."

"Is it time for the cake?" said Oaf, leaping to her feet.

"Yes," said Mom, "and I think we're in for a treat. Your dad's made us a beauty."

While everyone bustled about getting candles and cake, Juliet caught a glimpse of herself in the mirror: no Band-Aids taped to her nails, no rash spreading across her face, and no anxious V hovering between her eyebrows. There was just a medium-sized girl with medium brown hair, regular-sized feet, and a very big smile. "I am a capable person," she said to herself. "I am a capable person who can handle any crisis."

And she was right.

Let the Worry Tree animals help you with your worries too!

On the following pages there is room for you to write down things that may be worrying you.

If this book does not belong to you, you can do these activities on a separate sheet of paper.

Wolfgang

Piers

Petronella

Dimitri

Gwyneth

Delia

the worry tree

Wolfgang the Wombat

Here's Wolfgang the wombat. He's looking after these
friend worries for me.

_____

_____

_____

_____

_____

_____

Petronella the Pig

Petronella the pig worries about school. These are some of the worries she takes care of for me.

_____

_____

_____

_____

_____

_____

Remember! If this book does not belong to you, you can do these activities on a separate sheet of paper.

Gwyneth the Goat

Gwyneth the goat makes me feel better when I'm sick.

_____

_____

_____

_____

_____

_____

Dimitri the Dog

When I'm worried about my family, Dimitri the dog looks after them for me.

_____

_____

_____

_____

_____

_____

Remember! If this book does not belong to you, you can do these activities on a separate sheet of paper.

Piers the Peacock

Piers the peacock is in charge of minding worries about things I've lost.

_____

_____

_____

_____

_____

_____

Delia the Duck

Delia the duck knows that it's hard to get used to change—changing houses, changing schools, even changing bedrooms.

Remember! If this book does not belong to you, you can do these activities on a separate sheet of paper.

The Hole in the Trunk

Sometimes I have worries that I can't describe. The Worry Tree has a special place for these too.

Draw your favorite
Worry Tree animal here—
or make up a new one!

Remember! If this book does not belong to you, you can do these
activities on a separate sheet of paper.

Acknowledgments

I would like to thank my family and friends for all their encouragement and support over the many years it has taken to bring this book to life. In particular, thanks go to my parents and sister, who listened to me speak of Juliet and Oaf so often, these characters became like members of our family; all those who read various drafts and provided me with invaluable feedback, in particular, Russell Talbot, Dave Rees, Kate Thorne, Sue Oliver, assorted members of the Harwood family, and Sean Hegarty; my young reviewers, Jamie-Lee Vandenberg, Ramon Garcia, and Frizzy Trebilcock, for their honesty and encouragement; my manuscript assessors, Ruth Starke for teaching me "show don't tell," Jennifer Dabbs for helping me polish up my book, and Virginia Lowe for her eagle editing eye and for putting me in touch with my agent; Maeve Judge for setting me on the right path; Barbara Weisner and the South Australian Writers' Centre for all the advice and support; Rebecca Purling and Mark Polkinghorne for providing a peaceful environment in which many plot breakthroughs occurred; Polly, their dog, for her unorthodox editorial contribution; and, finally, my agent, Sheila Drummond, my publisher, Zoe Walton, and the rest of the team at Random House Australia for their hard work, faith, and enthusiasm.